CRANKENSTEIN

FOR MY FATHER AND GRANDFATHER,
WHO SHOWED ME THAT COMEDY CAN
CONQUER CRANKY, EVERY TIME.
— SB

FOR MY PARENTS,
WHO PUT UP WITH MY CRANKINESS.
— DS

ABOUT THIS BOOK

EVERY MORNING DURING THE ENTIRE PRODUCTION OF THIS BOOK,
DAN SANTAT WOULD MAKE HIMSELF GOOD AND CRANKY BY DEPRIVING
HIMSELF OF COFFEE. HAVING JUST THE RIGHT AMOUNT OF CRANKINESS
WAS IMPERATIVE TO THIS PROJECT. HE ILLUSTRATED THE BOOK USING
ADOBE PHOTOSHOP, EVEN THOUGH HIS COMPUTER CRASHED ALL THE TIME.
DAN THEN DECIDED TO HAND-LETTER EVERY SINGLE WORD, NOT REALIZING
THERE WERE A *LOT* OF WORDS IN THIS BOOK.

CRANKENSTEIN IS THE EMBODIMENT OF DAN SANTAT'S PURE RAGE.

... AND HE DID IT ALL FOR YOU.

THE FOLLOWING MONSTERS CONTRIBUTED TO THE MAKING OF THIS BOOK

EDITOR: CONNIE "NOSFERATHSU" HSU
ART DIRECTOR AND DESIGNER: DAVE "CHUPACAPLAN" CAPLAN
PRODUCTION MANAGER: CHARLOTTE "TRANSYLVEANEYIA" VEANEY
PRODUCTION EDITOR: MARTHA "CIPOLDEMORT" CIPOLLA

ISBN 978-0-545-90176-5

TEXT COPYRIGHT © 2013 BY SAMANTHA BERGER.
ILLUSTRATIONS COPYRIGHT © 2013 BY DAN SANTAT. ALL RIGHTS RESERVED.
PUBLISHED BY SCHOLASTIC INC., 557 BROADWAY, NEW YORK, NY 10012,
BY ARRANGEMENT WITH LITTLE, BROWN BOOKS FOR YOUNG READERS,
A DIVISION OF HACHETTE BOOK GROUP, INC. SCHOLASTIC AND ASSOCIATED
LOGOS ARE TRADEMARKS AND/OR REGISTERED TRADEMARKS OF SCHOLASTIC INC.

12 11 10 9 8 7 6 5 4 3 2 1   15 16 17 18 19 20/0

PRINTED IN THE U.S.A.   08

THIS EDITION FIRST PRINTING, SEPTEMBER 2015

CRANKENSTEIN

WRITTEN by
SAMANTHA BERGER

ILLUSTRATED by
DAN SANTAT

SCHOLASTIC INC.

HAVE YOU SEEN CRANKENSTEIN?

OH, YOU WOULD *TOTALLY*
KNOW IF YOU HAD.

YOU WOULD SAY,
GOOD MORNING!!
HOW ARE YOU?

YOU WOULD SAY,
WHO WANTS PANCAKES?
AUXIER
MAPLE SYRUP
IT'S FROM CANADA, EH!
EMPTY

YOU WOULD SAY,

TIME FOR

SCHOOL!

CRANKENSTEIN WOULD SAY,

MEHHHRRRR!!!

YOU MIGHT SEE CRANKENSTEIN WHEN IT'S SUPER RAINY OUTSIDE...

OR WHEN IT'S EXTRA COLD ON HALLOWEEN...

OR WHEN IT'S WAY TOO HOT FOR POPSICLES.

ESPECIALLY WHEN IT'S WAY TOO HOT FOR POPSICLES.

YOU CAN BE SURE TO FIND CRANKENSTEIN IN A LONG, LONG LINE.

CRANKENSTEIN *HATES* LONG, LONG LINES.

OR WHEN IT'S TIME TO TAKE GROSS COUGH SYRUP.

CRANKENSTEIN *HATES* GROSS COUGH SYRUP.

AND YOU'LL *DEFINITELY* SEE CRANKENSTEIN WHEN YOU SAY IT'S BEDTIME.

CRANKENSTEIN *HATES* WHEN YOU SAY IT'S BEDTIME.

MEHHRRR!

YES, THAT CRANKENSTEIN IS SOME PRETTY SCARY BUSINESS, ALL RIGHT.

BUT JUST WHEN YOU THINK THAT MONSTER IS HERE TO STAY...

HE MIGHT DO SOMETHING THAT SURPRISES YOU. BECAUSE WHEN CRANKENSTEIN MEETS *ANOTHER* CRANKENSTEIN...

IT JUST MIGHT MAKE HIM...

...AT LEAST FOR NOW.

...BUT DEFINITELY NOT TODAY.

WHEN CRANKY KIDS
HAVE MONSTROUS DAYS.

SCHOLASTIC

www.scholastic.com

Cover art by Dan Santat
Cover design by Dan Santat and Dave Caplan
Cover © 2013 Hachette Book Group, Inc.

ISBN 978-0-545-90176-5

$5.99

50

EAN

9 780545 901765